# Leaf Dance

For Mom and Dad —B.P.

SIMON SPOTLIGHT
An imprint of Simon & Schuster Children's Publishing Division
1230 Avenue of the Americas
New York, New York 10020
This Simon Spotlight edition October 2015
For information about special discounts for bulk purchases, please contact Simon & Schuster Special Sales at
1-866-506-1949 or business@simonandschuster.com
Manufactured in the United States of America 0915 LAK
2 4 6 8 10 9 7 5 3 1
Library of Congress Cataloging-in-Publication Data
Pearlman, Bobby.
Leaf dance / by Bobby Pearlman ; illustrated by Kathryn Mitter.
p. cm. — (Ready-to-read) (Classic Raggedy Ann & Andy)
Summary: Raggedy Ann, Raggedy Andy, and the other toys throw a party to celebrate the first day of fall.
[1. Dolls—Fiction. 2. Toys—Fiction. 3. Autumn—Fiction. 4. Parties—Fiction.]
I. Mitter, Kathy, ill. II. Title. III. Series. IV. Series: Classic Raggedy Ann & Andy
PZ7.P31658 Le 2001
[E]—dc21
2001029251
ISBN 978-1-4814-5083-6 (hc)
ISBN 978-1-4814-5082-9 (pbk)
ISBN 978-1-4814-5084-3 (eBook)
RaggedyAnnBooks.com

# RAGGEDY ANN & ANDY
## Leaf Dance

by Bobby Pearlman
illustrated by Kathryn Mitter

Ready-to-Read

Simon Spotlight
New York    London    Toronto    Sydney    New Delhi

"It is the first day of fall!"
yelled Raggedy Andy.
"Let's have a party!"

The dolls went outside.
The air was cold.
It was a perfect fall day.

Fido barked and ran in circles.

He loved a party.

"Let's pick some apples,"
Raggedy Ann said.
So they did.

Raggedy Ann and the Camel with the
Wrinkled Knees saw a scarecrow.
The cold wind blew
his arms and legs.
It looked like he was dancing!
Raggedy Andy saw the leaves
blowing.

"Let's have a leaf dance party!"
he said.
"May I come?" asked a big
orange pumpkin.

"I cannot dance,
but I can decorate!" he said.
Raggedy Ann hugged Pumpkin.
"Of course you may come!" she said.

The dolls saw some Leaf Fairies.

"We are going to have a leaf dance,"
Raggedy Andy said.

"May we come?"
asked the Leaf Fairies.

"Yes, do come," Little
Brown Bear said.

"Leaf dances are so much fun!"
The Leaf Fairies tickled a big tree.
The tree laughed
and her leaves floated down.

"Look," Raggedy Ann said.
"Each leaf is different."
One leaf was long, one was short,
some had points,
and some were round.

"Each leaf is a different
color, too," said Raggedy Andy.
One leaf was brown, one was red,
some were yellow,
and some were green.

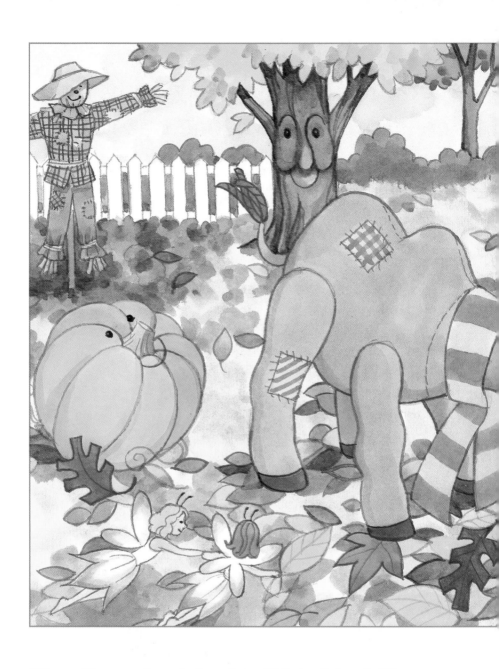

The Camel with the Wrinkled Knees
stepped on some leaves.

CRUNCH!
They smelled sweet!

Little Brown Bear
gave each doll an apple.
Uncle Clem put Pumpkin next
to the big tree.
The dolls made a big pile of leaves.
Fido and Henny jumped into it.

"Whee!" the Leaf Fairies cried
as leaves floated down.

The leaves were dancing!
The dolls danced with them.

Uncle Clem danced with Frederika.
Raggedy Ann hugged Pumpkin.
Henny danced with Cleety the Clown.

Raggedy Andy and Little Brown Bear
spun around.

"I love the first day of fall!"
cheered Raggedy Andy.
"We love leaf dances!"
cried the Leaf Fairies and the dolls.
"And I love all of you!"
said Raggedy Ann.